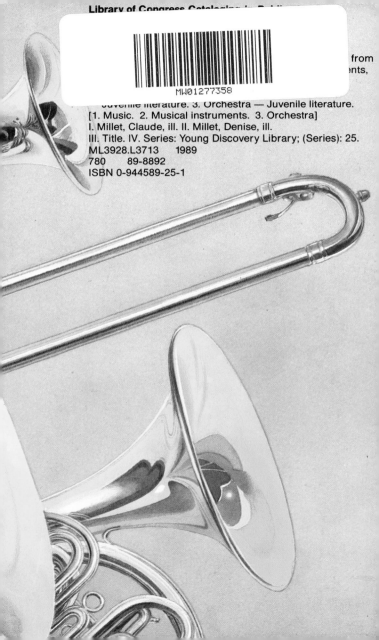

Library of Congress Cataloging in Publi...

...from
...ents,

...Juvenile literature. 3. Orchestra — Juvenile literature.
[1. Music. 2. Musical instruments. 3. Orchestra]
I. Millet, Claude, ill. II. Millet, Denise, ill.
III. Title. IV. Series: Young Discovery Library; (Series): 25.
ML3928.L3713   1989
780   89-8892
ISBN 0-944589-25-1

Written by Geneviève Laurencin
Illustrated by Claude and Denise Millet

Specialist Adviser:
Alain Duault
Musicologist

ISBN 0-944589-25-1
First U.S. Publication 1989 by
Young Discovery Library
217 Main St. • Ossining, NY 10562

©*Editions Gallimard, 1988*
Translated by Vicki Bogard
English text © *Young Discovery Library*

YOUNG DISCOVERY LIBRARY

Music!

YOUNG DISCOVERY LIBRARY

Listen!

Water rushing, leaves rustling, birds singing...nature is full of sounds! Some are loud and strong, others soft and sweet. You can be a musician too: whistle! sing! shout! Hit a coconut with a wooden spoon. Bang on some tin cans! A hollow reed makes music. So does a bow made of wood and string, with an empty can tied on.
Invent your own instruments.

There are three main families of instruments: percussion, string, and wind.

Do you have a xylophone? Tap each bar to make a different sound. **The xylophone is a percussion instrument.**

It is a fun way to learn the notes of the scale: do, re, mi, fa, sol, la, ti, do. Then you can play a song!

Not all percussion instruments produce distinct notes.

Some, like the big bass drum, only make loud, heavy thuds.

These 17th-century timpani could be tuned higher or lower by tightening the skin on top.

Snare drum, triangle, cymbals, gong, and vibraphone...these are just some members of the percussion family.

Percussion instruments produce sounds when struck with drumsticks, mallets or hands.

The first musical instruments were probably from the percussion family. They set the beat, but also add new sound textures.

Shake the maracas...tap the claves...scrape the güiro...click the castanets! These instruments from Spain and Latin America add excitement to music.

Percussion around the world

Drums set a beat or a mood.
In the Central African nation
of Burundi, these log-drummers
announce the planting season.
Then they put their drums away
until the following year.

The balafon is a West African
xylophone used to accompany dancers.

The Ko drum plays an
important role in
Chinese theater, where
drumbeats have special
meanings.

In Japan, Kodos are both
athletes and musicians.
According to legend, gods
are trapped inside a giant
drum. If the Kodos
hit the drum hard
enough, the gods
will be set
free. Then
there will
be rain and
sun upon
the earth.

14

The violin is the best known member of the string family.

A wooden bow, strung with horsehair, is drawn across the violin's strings to produce sounds.

The crwth (krŏŏth) was a bowed lyre played in England and Wales.

Minstrels played this instrument in the Middle Ages.

The first violin was made in the mid-1500's. Its parents were the viols. Some viols were held on the arm. Others, like the viola da gamba, were held between the knees, as this French musician is doing. Viols were played before rich lords, while the violin was used for common dancing. Today the violin has the lead part in an orchestra.

Viola da gamba

The tools of the luthier

This violin may look simple, but violin-making is an art that takes skill and patience. The **luthier** cuts out, shapes, glues, drills, sands, assembles and varnishes over 70 pieces of fine woods to make a violin. Then he strings it with four strings of steel-wound gut. The **bow-maker** makes a bow by attaching about 150 horsehair threads to a wooden stick. Only the tail hair, from white Canadian or Siberian stallions, is long enough to be used!

In the Italian city of Cremona, Antonio Stradivari (1648-1737) made beautiful violins. Today a 'stradivarius' is worth a fortune!

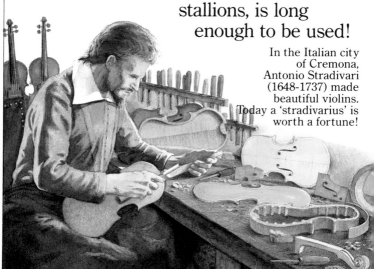

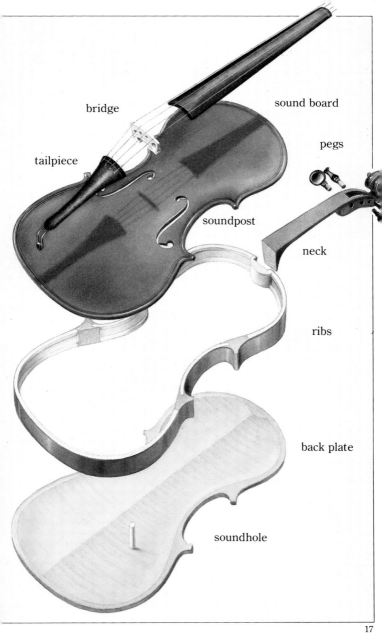

bridge

sound board

pegs

tailpiece

soundpost

neck

ribs

back plate

soundhole

The harp has 46 strings. Why isn't it part
of the string family?
Because it is not played with a bow!

The string family:

violin

viola

cello

bass

A chamber ensemble: the string quartet
usually has 2 violins, 1 viola, 1 cello,
but no bass.

Shorter strings, higher sounds.

The violin, with its short thin strings, produces high, sweet sounds.
The longer and thicker the string, the deeper its sound.
With its long, fat strings the bass can sound like a thunderstorm!

Dancing-masters had tiny violins they could carry in their coat pockets!

**Pipes to blow into: those are
the wind instruments.** Prehistoric
man made flutes from bones.

bone flute (1,000 BC)

Panpipes are made of hollow
reeds which are cut
and tied together.

Then, in China, panpipes made
of different-sized reeds
appeared. The shortest reed
has the highest sound; the
longest has the lowest.
Wind instruments are divided
into two groups:
woodwinds and
brass.

Two early
instruments: the
sackbut, a brass,
and the shawm,
a woodwind.

The brass family is loud and clear! Brass bands are seen in most parades. The army uses bugles because they can be heard from far away.

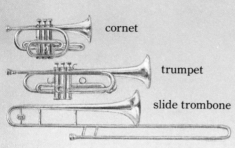

French horn

cornet

trumpet

slide trombone

A New Orleans street band

Moving a trombone's **slide**, or a trumpet's **valves**, lets a musician play different notes. The movement makes the air column inside the horn longer or shorter. A player can also stretch his lips to change the sound.

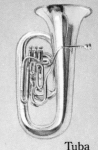

Tuba

24

To play a recorder, you blow into the hole at the top end.

Woodwinds are not all made of wood.
But they are all pipes with holes in them, with one hole to blow into. The **recorder** is a woodwind that is not hard to learn to play.

To play a flute, you blow air across the top of the hole.

Use your fingers to cover all the holes: when you blow into it, you will hear a low sound. Now take your fingers away, one by one. The column of air gets shorter, the sound is higher.

piccolo

oboe

clarinet

bassoon

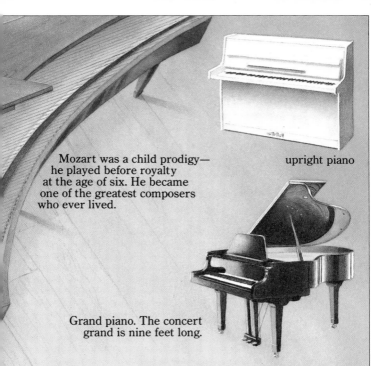

upright piano

Mozart was a child prodigy—
he played before royalty
at the age of six. He became
one of the greatest composers
who ever lived.

Grand piano. The concert
grand is nine feet long.

The piano can play sweet melodies,
crashing chords, and everything
in between!
How does it work?
When you press a **key**, it causes
a felt hammer to hit strings,
and you hear the note. The pedals
soften or hold the sound. With
seven **octaves**, or levels, you
can make a wide range of sounds.
Learning to play an instrument
with 88 keys is, indeed, hard.

Here is the orchestra! It brings together strings, brass, woodwinds and percussion...all in a magical mix. Can you count them all?

snare drum

xylophone

bass drum

French horns

trumpets

harp

flutes

oboes

first violins

second violins

The conductor sets the mood of a piece and helps the musicians play together.

timpani

triangle

cymbals

tubas

trombones

clarinets

bassoons

bass

violas

cellos

There are many kinds of orchestras in other countries. Eastern and Western musicians borrow from each other.

In Japan, Gagaku, or court music, is played with very old instruments. Here are the koto, oboe, drum and flute. It is said that the koto sounds like a dragon on the beach, talking to the waves...

a gamelan

The gamelan is a Balinese orchestra.
It plays for singing, dancing and
puppet shows. There are over 2,000
gamelans on the island of Bali!
The instruments shown are the
gong-chimes and the xylophone.

This trio from India is made up
of a sitar (right), a tambura
(center), and a tabla, or pair
of tuned drums.
Indian music may sound odd or
funny to you. But the music
is very complex. To master
the **rhythms** takes many years
of study.

Jazz was born in New Orleans, around the 1900's. It was a meeting, a joining, of African rhythms and Western instruments.
Jazz is called the voice and soul of the black experience in America. When playing, the musicians pick a **theme** and **improvise** on it.

An electric guitar—the main instrument of rock 'n' roll music.

New sounds, new music!

With electronic instruments the possibilities for new sounds are endless. Mixers and amplifiers replace valves and air.

Musical oddities

In both modern and ancient times, musicians have tried to improve on their instruments, or invent new ones. Dizzy Gillespie, the jazz musician, is well-known for the odd angle of his trumpet's tube.

A 17th-century French serpent. It was curved to make the fingering easier.

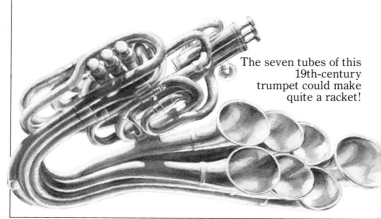

The seven tubes of this 19th-century trumpet could make quite a racket!

The harp-lyre was invented in 1827. It is not a harp, but a large guitar with three necks.

Modern composers use all kinds of common objects in their music. Typewriters, cow bells and chains are used to make sounds... even car horns and old wash boards.

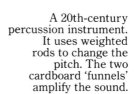

A 20th-century percussion instrument. It uses weighted rods to change the pitch. The two cardboard 'funnels' amplify the sound.

Oh, me name is MacNamara,
I'm the leader of the band.
Although we're few in number
we're the finest in the land.

We play at wakes and weddings
and very fancy balls,
and when we play at funerals
we play the March from Saul.

Oh, the drums go banging, the
cymbals clanging, and the horns
they blaze away.
McCarthy pumps the old bassoon
while I the pipes do play.

Index